tiny owl publishing

Persian text and Illustration Copyright © 2013 Chekkeh Publication
This edition © 2015 Tiny Owl Publishing Ltd
1 Repton House, Charlwood Street, SW1V 2LD, London, UK

Translated by Azita Rassi
Persian collection editor: Ali Seidabadi
Graphic designer: Elahe Javanmard

The moral right of Susan Taghdis as the author and Ali Mafakheri as the
illustrator has been asserted.

ISBN 978-1-910328-10-1

A catalogue record of this book is available from the British Library
www.tinyowl.co.uk

Tiny Owl Publishing Ltd,
Registered in England No. 08297587

The Snowman and the Sun

Susan Taghdis

Ali Mafakheri

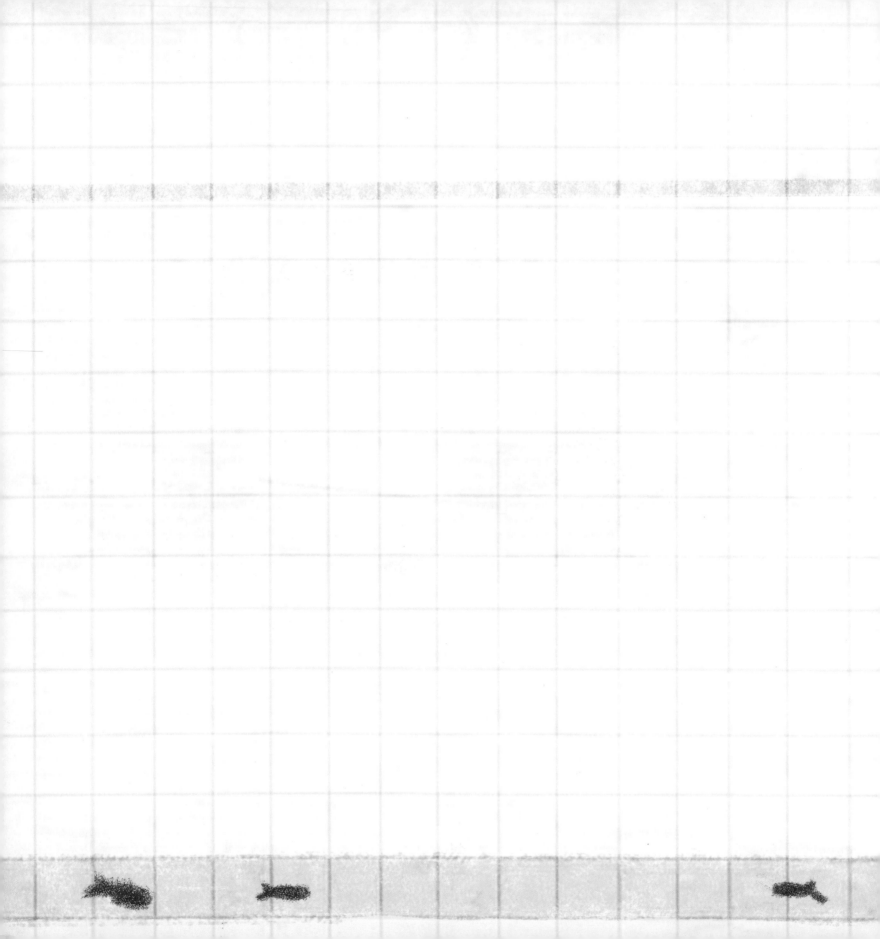

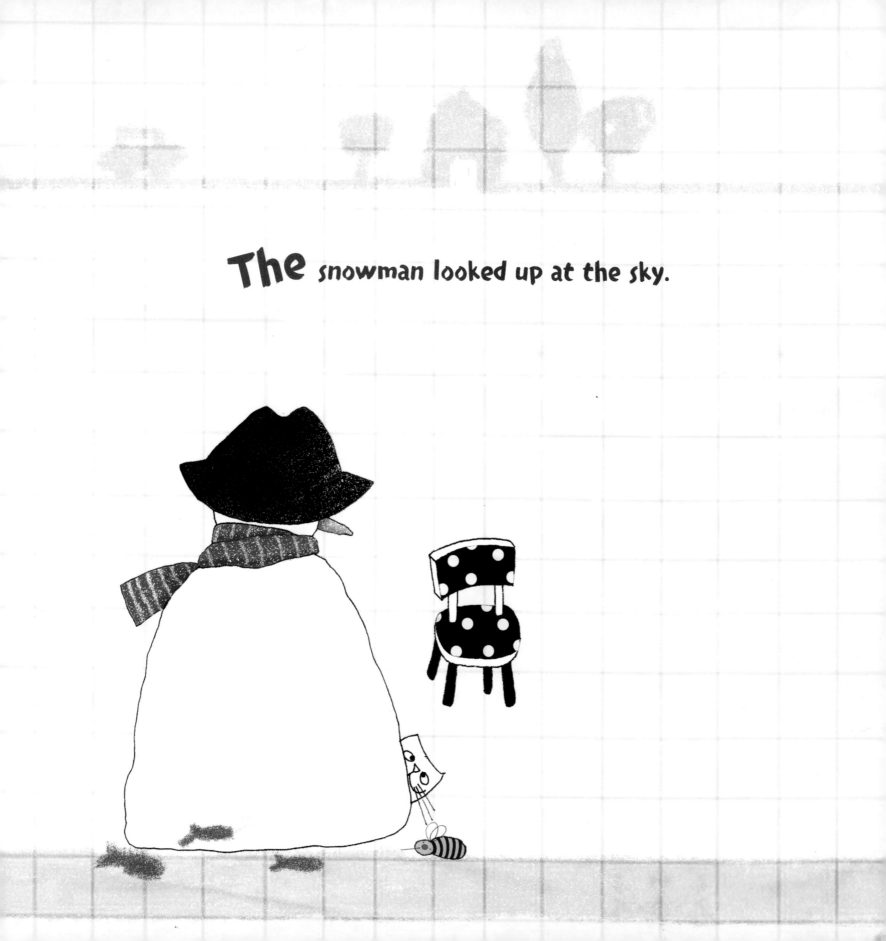

The snowman looked up at the sky.

Way up high, the sun laughed. "Phew, what a warm sun!" said the snowman. "What happens if I melt?"

The snowman melted and transformed into water.

The snowman ran as
water over the ground.

The ground tickled him. "What warm ground!" said the watery snowman. "I wonder if I will evaporate?"

The snowman changed from water to tiny little water droplets, floating up and up.

Then he looked at the sky and said, "Birds are so lucky." Then he kept going up into the cold sky until he became a cloud.

The cloud was free, drifting around in the sky. He
went this way and that. "What a nice sky! But what if
it gets cold and I turn to snow and fall down?"

The air then started to get colder. The snowman felt chilly as a cloud. Little by little, he turned back into snow and floated back down to the ground, flake by flake.

The next day when the children woke up, the ground was covered with snow.

The snowman, from his big drift of snow, recognized the child looking out of his window.

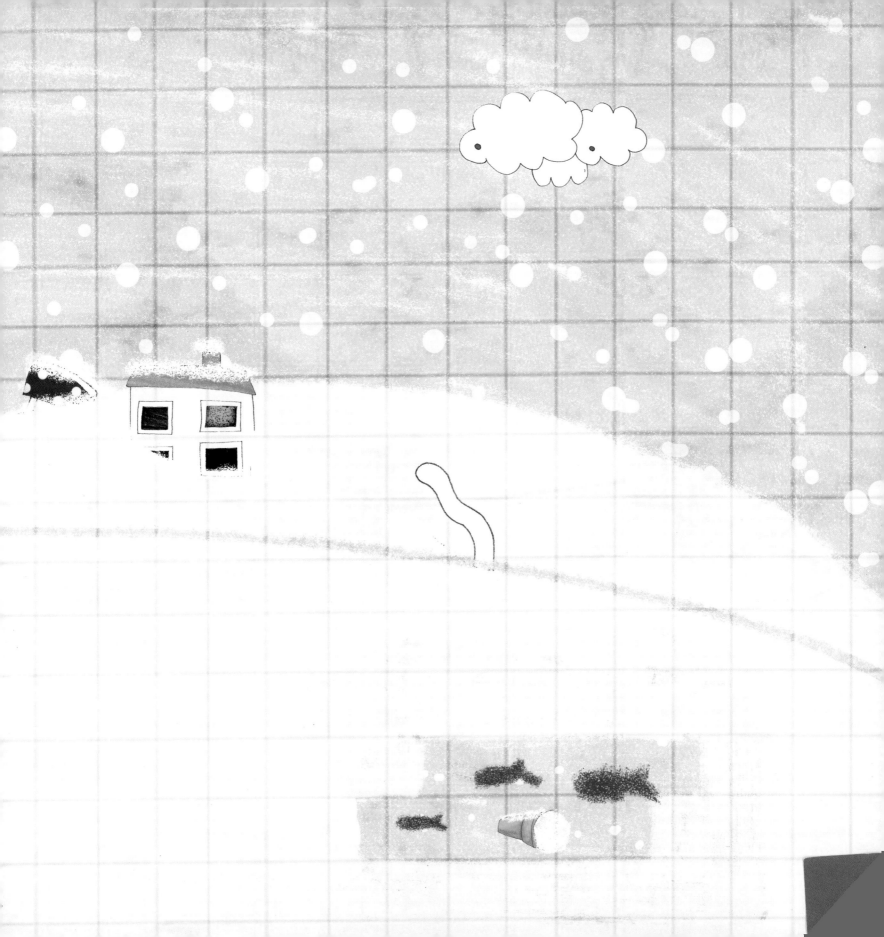

It was the same boy that had turned him into a snowman in the first place. He winked at the boy from the snow and said, "Make a snowman of me!"

Later, the snowman looked up at the sky,
waiting for the sun to appear.